"I love this book so much! The subject matter is [...] such a creative way to introduce this information to them...I loved the bright and playful artwork." – Faatima Harley (Chocolate Yoga Destinations)

"I read this story...it has great intent and is very positive and encouraging for all boys...I love the multicultural theme." – Oni Lasana (Storyteller)

"This book is needed. It teaches all kids how to handle pressure, while teaching younger kids their ABCs in a fun and memorable way. My son loves it." - Keyairra C. (Parent)

"It is a building block of positive reinforcement for a child's character when they begin their journey of life. I have a two-year-old godson and this book inspired me on so many levels as an adult. Once I read his book to him repeatedly, it will serve as a constant motivation for him that he is special, and he can be whatever he wants to be at a very early age." - Derek S.

"I like the book. It is simple and easy to comprehend. It is colorful. A very creative way to learn the alphabet. Each letter and picture combine very well. The book tells a story within itself through the alphabet." - Lowell T.

This was so cute. I loved it. It felt warm & authentic." - Aimee J.

"This book is motivational. It encourages you to acknowledge your feelings and other people's feelings and teaches you how to meditate." - Taedyn B. (11-year-old reader)

"Cute, Incisive & Necessary" - Jordan C.

Boys Breathe: An ABC Introduction to Self-Confidence

Copyright © 2022 by Keesha Dancy

Written by Keesha Dancy and Kaiden Jones

First Edition February 2022

ISBN: 978-1-957102-00-9 (Paperback)
ISBN: 978-1-957102-02-3 (eBook)

Library of Congress Control Number: 2021924205

Pearled Butterfly Publishing, LLC
1910 Madison Ave #2284
Memphis, TN 38104

www.pearledbutterflypublishing.com

For special orders, wholesale sales, or bulk orders, contact:
CustomerService@PearledButterflyPublishing.com

BOYS BREATHE:

AN ABC INTRODUCTION TO SELF-CONFIDENCE

WRITTEN BY
KEESHA DANCY AND
KAIDEN JONES

ILLUSTRATED BY
UZMA GHAURI

DEDICATION

Dedicated to all boys around the world; my Mommy and Daddy, who always love me "more" and support me in all my adventures; my Mimi, who is always there for me and takes me around the world; Pawpaw Russell; Grandma Lisa & Papa Kelvin; and my great grandparents (Grandpa Curtis and Grandma Stine, Nana LaVerne, Granny and Granddad). Thank you all for loving and encouraging me. I love you to infinity! ~ Kaiden

This book is dedicated to my grandsons, Gabriel and Kaiden (the inspiration for this book); my aunt Dondi (thank you for that extra push); my godson, Maurcellus; and all boys who do not yet know they are the future. You are loved, you are special, and you can do anything that you put your mind to do because ALL things are possible, and the World is Your Oyster! Remember, YOU ARE AMAZING!

~ Mimi Keesha

I am unique, and so are you.

This book was created for us; you, too!

To remind us of how special we are.

We can press forward and set the bar.

We are loved, we are worthy, and we are enough!

It is okay to express our feelings when times get tough.

This book is filled with positive affirmations.

Because at times, we need a break to practice meditation.

Breathe in, breathe out, then count to ten.

Think happy thoughts and find your Zen!

"What's wrong, Sebastian?" Cheng asks.

"I'm having a bad day," Sebastian says.

"I understand how you feel. When I have a bad day, I talk about my feelings with my friends or teacher. Sometimes, I think about something funny," Gabriel says.

"When I am sad, I draw," Cheng says.

Amari chimes in, "When I have a bad day, I meditate. Let me show you how.

Close your eyes and think about the sun. Start from ten and count down to one.

Take a deep breath in through your nose, pull it in deep all the way from your toes.

Now hold that breath to the count of three, while thinking about your favorite tree."

Closing, Gabriel adds, "Blow that same breath out through your mouth, nice and slow."

"Now, isn't that a breeze? Repeat after me. Ready, let's go."

A

I AM AMAZING

EVERYTHING I DO IS GREAT.

AMAZING

BRAVE

FRIENDLY

HANDSOME

INQUISITIVE

LOVED

MINDFUL

OPTIMISTIC

POSITIVE

SMART

CREATIVE

WINNER

UNIQUE

VICTORIOUS

TALENTED

I AM QUICK

I AM ZEALOUS

I AM FULL OF ENERGY AND PASSION FOR WHAT I LOVE. WE ALL HAVE A PURPOSE THAT COMES FROM ABOVE.

"Hey, amigo, now how do you feel?" Gabriel asks.
"This was fun! I feel so much better now," Sebastian says.
"Remember, buddy, you are not alone. There is always
 someone to talk to," Amari says.
"Thank you, friends," Sebastian replies.
"I am amazing, I am brave, I am creative."
The boys chant in unison as they head home.

ABOUT THE AUTHORS

Keesha Dancy, a native of East Saint Louis, IL, currently resides in Memphis, TN. Keesha is a U.S. Army Retired Soldier, current substitute teacher, and the founder of All Things Are Possible, Inc., a nonprofit organization committed to empower and inspire youth through Travel, Education, Mentorship, and Service. Keesha earned her Bachelor of Science Degree in Resources Management from Troy University and her MBA (Human Resource Management) from Columbia Southern University. Keesha uses the core lessons she has discovered from her life's journey and experiences to educate, engage, and empower today's youth. Her passion for empowering children comes forward in her storytelling. Keesha's hobbies include reading, crafting, and giving back to her community. She also enjoys spending time with her family, friends, and mini poodle, Gucci. Keesha is an avid traveler, she's traveled the world to over 50 countries and counting. Her favorite travel buddies are her grandsons. Find out more about Keesha by following her on FB at Keesha Dancy-Author and IG @keeshadancyauthor. You can also contact her via email keeshaldancy@gmail.com for school visits and/or speaking engagements.

Kaiden Jones is an inquisitive and active 8-year-old third grader; his favorite subjects are Science and English. Kaiden's hobbies include track, soccer, and video games. Kaiden has a soft spot for animals and is a nurturer by nature. He aspires to serve the community as a police officer or veterinarian. Kaiden was inspired to write this book to "show people what they can be and to teach other children how to meditate and be calm." Kaiden's passion for reading, traveling, and journaling makes him the perfect co-author.

Made in the USA
Columbia, SC
09 April 2022